I0625613

Turn Left at November

poems by

Wendy Rathbone

Turn Left at November
Poems by Wendy Rathbone
Copyright © 2015 by Wendy Rathbone
Published by Eye Scry Publications
www.eyescrypublications.com
All Rights Reserved

ISBN: 978-1-942415-08-4
Eye Scry Publications

Many other Eye Scry Publications are available at a substantial volume discount to bookstores, libraries, etc. Please visit our website at
www.eyescrypublications.com

For Della
fellow traveler of my autumn thoughts

Contents

Turn Left at November

On Stopping for Directions

through north's tall door
turn left at November
wade leaf on leaf
toward the waking moon
you will find it

December's End

Light folds upon the window
sparking rain with gold
   The slender moon dissolves
   like damp sugar

The trodden city of December is gone
   her faerie fires
   and fake red sleighs
   her gypsy trees
   and ginger mansions

Winter wades upon the wind
   wandering, calling
   searching

Someone lost
someone far from home

just January's elf
   looking for his ice-bed

Winter's Shelf

hidden pathways to the moon
the north's blue breath
star-rise
amethyst dusks
winter wind bottled
and sold here

Night Servants

Careful
there are night servants about
still setting out the stars
balancing the un-dusted moon
combing the land for wind
shadow treading in the deeps

Take the cold and thread it
through the trees
November waits for snow
the way I wait
with my candle
for you to meet me
through the leaves that fall
and keep falling
on our jackets
and into our open hands

Unmaking Autumn

Out at the excavation site
where they are taking apart autumn
leaf by fabled leaf
the searchlights try to catch us
putting the eyes back into the pumpkins
the moon back in the witch-shaped sky
We steal blood kisses
behind the naked apple orchards

Don't

Don't look like that
It's a devil of an autumn this year
matching your nacarine eyes
Leaves whirl
and you have me running for cover
away from your gatherings
your basket
I won't be collected
left on a shelf to die
Don't smile
Don't put your hand in my hair
Don't

Back from the Dead

The sky has amnesia tonight
forgetting the moon
This is the way it works
Memory rises in the east
a purple light
Your eyes were like the miles
I'd traveled
the valleys of curses and shame
You told me I didn't exist
but I never forgot
the bewitching brush
of your corporeal kiss

Outlook

This December
acorns concern me
and the dark golden leaf of the closing
year
Where are you hiding?
Under the cactus trees
my buried soul
Keep the curtains closed, please
This atmosphere of ghosts
the wretched winter stars like henchmen
always watching
Leave me to my canopy of shadows
The air is brilliant
with salt and dust glitter and snow
Ask me your fortune
I am inside the crystal ball
trying to come through
and tell you
the outlook is not promising

Shivering

shivering the moon from my shoulders
I say to November
let me in your cloud scrap home
breathe the knife of you
taste your chimney-smoke and rain
your damp-armed trees
and all their rag-patch sheddings
that quilt the land

Poem of a Vampire

diamond rain from the stars
headdress of sky
worn by the wild moon
I am autumn sent to the grave
leaf hair and pine-cone heart
a witch-doll body
a winter coat
open a vein of silver wind
I'll speak in a voice of bone
31 days of October
drip into my mouth
apples echoes red sleet
now I sit in your shadow
knees drawn under my sleeves
while the topaz days
slowly age you
into my dust-folk land

December Phantom

Rain batters what's left
of December's leaves
torturing the earth
killing dust
All the black creeks fill
The night is broken
by your darker touch

Love Song to Autumn

The hours are putting together the season
hammering, then letting the beaten silence
pray

Thrown down by the stars
the red air is in a panic
of October

Simultaneously I can
love you and forsake you
in endless smoke curtaining
the tender dying hills
The dancing fate of the wind
plays songs that hurt
and burn the long grass

I want you
but I don't know how to cage the firmament
I don't know how to paint the fight of you

November watches you build
broken souls with a darker gaze
forcing the trees to kneel
the snow to execute its white days

I know of no hell where you are
cider in my cup sweetening
I drink to you by the
golden window
My mouth holds all your tears

What They Say

the street says
  I lead to all rainstorms
the window says
  light, come be my poem
the lamp says
  I want to be the silk sun
the moon says
  make me a cape of dark rivers
the stars say
  longing keeps us apart
the wind says
  I hear the cities crumbling
the poem says
  light, linger at my window
the autumn says
  this is my planet of candles and lace
the vampire says
  there is fog in my hair
the robot says
  why don't you write in the margins
the phantom says
  adorn me in lasers and photons
the oracle says
  everything is impossible
the sea says
  deepen the flux, salt the bend
the sky says

    double back on me so we will be face to
face
the dusk says
    the suicide of the sun is my favorite
time of day
the night says
    I am the texture of obsidian glass
the dream says
    walk to me along the starry rim
outer space says
    pour me a glass of astronauts
the candle-flame says
    I am a gold leaf made of light

Always

passing by the moon-lamps of
the night boulevard
all the newly naked trees
the autumn princes
bathing in the golden dark
orange eyes and wicked grins
the sky pours
whiskey stars
under the drunken leaves
the deep damp chill
is always
somebody's ghost

For Lovers Only

heaped with flowers and candles
the boat on the orange lake
is for lovers only
those who watch buildings melt
see unicorns in the city
those who wander among
the hands of trees
who paint their houses blue
who see faces in the water's surface
and know this hour is fire
is a serenade of all
that is true

It Happened

it happened to me
just the rambling of wind
of weather
of time
the pens the paper
needing to trap the now
which is everything
when it breaks
liquid stars pour in
if you listen you can hear them
the nights of years
walking down the bent galactic arms
on cold shard legs
unbalanced
it happened
the trees becoming starships holding
candles
far into a red-drenched evening
where the strings of
my body
pull me on

Tonight, Summer

pink and graphite clouds tonight
summer comes heavy
not like winter crystal air
so thin it can shatter
but with a fog-weighted moon
low enough to jump
I put my hands into the mix of dark sky
they travel far
the wind sounds like a ray-gun
from an old science fiction movie
I drink motionless lemonade
glitter air resting on the glass
moth-wings powdering the hours
and finally sleep beneath
the floating ash of stars

The Master

in cold hills
where light pinks the snow
touching the sky
the immortal lives
he has learned to breathe past age
underneath the paragraphs of years
his story thinning out
until it cannot be touched
molded pasted compelled
or hung like a shell of a star
waiting to burn out

November Stillness

November stillness
an asphyxiation of the waking day
something of the criminal plays
in your eyes
disorder and secrets
as night smothers half the world
Autumn begins the dust
grooms the wilted
spreads the red
silvers the stars
These long evenings
when you skulk beyond
the candle's reach

Storms

Storms
and your backstreet eyes
blades
caught in sodium's gold
under a ruined moon
I yank and the shadows
yank back
A cottage of mist
This is what you offer?
Leather and cologne and vanity
Still I call you
my voice like gravel mixing
with the deadend of November
I am shaking and treacherous
I want to say
there is poison in your smile
because
I put it there

Six Haiku

old shadows
the wind's
pipesmoke taste

#

thunder
invisible starships
on Wednesday's green horizon

#

wolf-wind
autumn spells of
all the witch books ever written

#

swirl of fall leaves
wild pages
of fairy diaries

#

chattering
amongst themselves
dead leaves

#

moon-rise
shadows meet
my muse

Silence Ravishing

Snow-etched silence
ravishing darkness
your hair like December evening
The sullen moon hangs
just off the edge of sanity
You own me with a look
I can't even finish my paperwork
The distractions of winter
and you

Auburn Pages

in this sighing season
the auburn pages of sky drift
soon the moon-man
casting his silver lines
will settle back to dust
the stars will make soft radio sounds

Gold

Come fall
the leaf-eyed poet
drapes his rants of gold
on bare branches under the moon
You can taste
a hundred years of dusk-drenched lanes
the glass skies of September
cracking
All fires turn blue
Cold beauty rules
the thrusting distances
between stars
Sometimes the night says
I am your true body
but so faraway

Book of Autumn

notes of a silver sky
star blind snow
my breath erases the moon
I can't go on
I lift the dipper of space
to my lips
all the windows drip black leaves
I want to live in a book of autumn poems
in walls of numbered pages
where I will fill them
with derelict words
gravity and time

Letter to Orion

in the silt of stars
you walk
I am the girl in the back of the class
you are filled with
the slickness of night
I twirl my rings on my fingers
how many ruins of time slip through
you?
nobody sees me
your three fiend fathers
abandoned you long ago
I too have no one
only the burning moonships of my
dreams
like an offering of jewels
floating toward you

Dust

The wind is made of ghosts,
of last century's dust
where ruined cities sink into
dunes of curled sleep.

End of the Game

I remove everything from the board
hotels, cards, chessmen, metal hats
the dots on the dice
I can hear you calling
from the mirror where I put you
in your favorite suit and tie
It's a spell you can't un-do
I kiss the glass
I am ribbons of myself blowing
all directions
reaching through the other side
and around unruly death
for the love I am currently
destroying

Tomorrow Street

The road swells skyward
distant, lanterned

Hidden curbs of time
keep captive the illusion
of order

but the road spreads everywhere
spilled ink trails uncontrolled
mixing space and moon-lamps
a maze a lunatic swirl
going any place and some when
a birdless unending sea
a night desert that never
meets dawn
sorrow's road where dreams
keep waking
within dreams
with teasing malice
looking inward
to the mind
of being

I'd Leave You

if you weren't so
golden
if you weren't always walking
on the light shards of broken stars
rummaging for love
I'd let you go
palm slipping out of yours
stinging with your salt
you who
stands in gathered shadows
like a fever
if you weren't so luminous
in your tatters of stardust
your flushed glamour
your grief for the
measureless beyond
I'd leave you

The Forever Guest

I am the dark crow of secret towns
the flurry of suns the moon's old hat
I am a hideous sylph swooning in
Neptune's lair
the golden android that hosts your soul
I am the future beaming
all the long hours drunk from the dusk
I am the forever guest in the
the rooms of your poems
lifting their skirts of dust

Wake Up

a dog begins
break of day
the worst time
distant trucks roar
I try to think of the sea
cold as blue winter
Don't wake up
Don't make me wake up

I Linger

I do not sleep fast
I linger and dream
chrome-crested rippling seas
the candles of gondolas
and a
crazy-eyed merman
with tongue of salt
and moonsong
fishing for bottled lost notes of
the drowned, the much-loved dead
who saw him first
with their white-bone eyes

All the Words

all the words I didn't write
come back now
out of the empty page
over the faded blue lines
like spirit poems
relic poems
cacodemon poems

The List

a planet
clinging to the wind
darkling autumn
in a bottle
the unfinished rafters of space
not for sale
my love
for
the green apple moon

Three Haiku

skeleton house
the end of
unhappy endings

#

peach-soft clouds
trains rustle
in the reddening fields

#

terrible muse
cloud-skulking tonight
moonlight the color of neglect

This Town

Well, this town on the rim of dust—
it's apocalyptic in autumn
when the dead come back
languidly kicking leaves
their annoying moonlit glances
I'm afraid to look at you
Maybe you won't know me
or you hate me now
I follow you quietly down the battered
road
Your soft velvet coat is like new
still smelling of laundry soap

Come To...

Come to the end
and let me un-do you

tangle you in my fingers
quest in your eyes

Long darks wrap
your heart

There is salt in you
I would shake

Dreams like snow
falling up

The ghost of you
a lily in my hand

Dear Poem

I look at you through phases of bearded
clouds
night-long
bending your arms like a galaxy
I've breathed you underwater
I've made your hair sea-green
I've watched tides of ink form you
I don't know who you are
but secrets sleep in you
psychologies lost minutes vampire
voices

I dreamt the burning colors of
slaked love
your tattoo-look in fashion
wolfthorn spiced
go get a little drunk now
as if you mean it
then look in the mirror and reverse
write yourself on my skin with static
become candled and iridescent
tongue made of suns suffocating in
lanterns
the black leather night wears you

I lean into your intrinsic air
your sea wrecks
your autumn furred dark
stony altars twin souls
golden rivers leading underworld
your salt roar grief
grotto of leaf and dust and foam

you
poem
do you remember tapestried sunsets
sequins in the sky
the moon talking
all evening until it fell into the Pacific
believe me when I say
I saw my dog's ghost
my future self
the blue starships of November

Rude

the vampire
sits on the couch
in his black tie
smelling of satin and cedar
watching me

House of Wind

rain of damp gold ballads
glamour of clouds
black lamps surrounding the moon
star-tufts
I open
a December window
the cold breaths of ice-ghosts
rush by
then stand silent in the parlor corners
dripping
my hands cup them
these unknown souls these owls
of winter
the spectacles of my house are askew
it has three eyes
through which my phantoms peer
the wine of muses froths
aroma of
ivy and northern seas

I asked you all here tonight
   the wind on the stair
   the irises of black stars
   the hands of water
   all the dust figments of my childhood
to share a bit of obliteration
a touch of the old moon wrinkling
in our sherry-glasses
to infuse you
pungent and quaking
on these hyper-journeys from
galaxy to galaxy
so drink to the void
to arsenals of suns
then drink to cold driftlight
pinkgold purplechrome vapors
illuminating
your jewel-lined way

Gone

the candles are gone from the
    windowsills
as you roam forever the
    soft silk hills
the stars all weep
caravans sleep
where the north wind wanders and chills

Alone in August

In midsummer
the doily moon drifts
across the Victorian sky.
The fog-silence settles low
on the hayfields.
I hear the distant call of onyx gods.
The all-black starships
hover close to
the encroaching edge of forever.
How
I miss you.

Things I Like

light's endless travelogue
each particle of dust a planet

this house this street
this galaxy

a moon rattling on the windowsill

the distant gold light of the lonely

autumn and space incinerating time

the stars lining up their flickering
momentums

wind chasing itself

a feeling as if I have unknown limbs
yet unhinged

short trees over blond grass overlapping
into endless spatial widths opening
incredible distances inside me

My Favorite Movie Scene Is...

not fogged moonbeams or
the blue of midnight eyes
or replicants crying for a soul
not the wet pavement mirroring
their shadows and their lightsuits
golden auroras in the trafficked night
not owls blinking pretending
to see them
not far-off music in the ruins
or air cars
or supertoy clowns and bears
or eyeliner melting
under thick wet bangs
or emergency sirens
or the song of memory
hiding in machine banks
not green rivers or citystorms
or iridescent sunrises
on tower windows
or exhaust steaming off
the autumn air
not this future no
most definitely not
this science fiction of noondreams
the alabaster purity of
artificial awareness
playing chess and hearts
robots in love

not doll heads floating
in violent sewers
not the whirl and tremble of
the blaster
lost children lost ships
lost worlds
dead cops dead synthetics
not doves flying away from
the disturbed poetry of androids
simply
the way he sits on the roof
in the rain

(tribute to "Blade Runner")

Three Words

in the ghost-swept skies
a dim bronze sun
dips down
into my book of poems
what if words
like million year-old insects
could be caught in amber?
I would wear
about my neck
these three:
shrewd northward cloak

The Month of October

If there is a god
  it is October
If there is an eternal soul
    mine is the longest dusk
    flared gold
    traveling to the furthest quasar
If there is hope
    it is in the candy-scented night
    where any wonder may be revealed

October sifts the stars
  causing them to glitter
October lights the candle moon
October reminds the mirror to reflect
October causes wind
October is the campfire where
    fortunes are told
October walks the rim of void
October wears patchwork

The language of shadow
wraps up all the witches and apples
and chuckling leaves. No more words
remain to speak of kid-spells
and magic mists, fire-brained pumpkins
and skull moons, clouds stretching like
spider-lace and bare trees birthing dryads,
scarecrows dreaming of Armani suits
and the marble-eyed owl blinking
and the knowledge that the spirit wears
more than human flesh.

The heart rules the muse.
And I say:
My heart is field-fog and ghost chill running
lonely, long and lost with the
rushing wind bound up
in pine and salt and guttering flame,
burnt wax and caramel breath…all spiraling
toward the center of my unseelie
soul.

There I live
in the elixirs
of October.

Publishing Credits

"On Stopping for Directions" was first published in Star*line and the Dwarf Stars Award 2011 anthology.

"December's End" was first published in Star*line.

"Shivering" was first published in One Sentence Poems.

"Dust" was first published in One Sentence Poems.

"old shadows" was first published in the Southern California Haiku Anthology.

"thunder" was first published in Scifikuest.

"wolf-wind" was first published in Scifikuest.

"swirl of fall leaves" was first published in Scifikuest.

"chattering" was first published in the Southern California Haiku Anthology.

"moon-rise" was first published in the Southern California Haiku Anthology.

"Come To…" was first published in Dreams and Nightmares.

"The Month of October" was first published in Star*line.

Wendy Rathbone

Since the mid-'80s Wendy Rathbone has had over 500
poems published in both mainstream and genre venues.
She's had seven chapbooks published from seven different
publishers and recently they were all gathered together in
an omnibus edition, "Unearthly," available on Kindle from
Amazon which also includes her first place award-
winning chapbook "Scrying the River Styx" from the
Anamnesis Press chapbook contest.

Wendy has been nominated over a dozen times for the Science Fiction Poetry Association's Rhysling Award, and for their Dwarf Star short-short poetry award. Her most recent work can be found in: Asimov's SF, Pedestal Magazine, Dreams and Nightmares, Scifikuest, Horror Writers of America Poetry Showcase, One Sentence Poems, Mythic Delirium, and more.

A brand new short story, "I Keep the Dark That is Your Pain," is also out in the pivotal 2015 anthology: A Darke Phantastique.

Her soft sf novel "Letters to an Android" is on Amazon Kindle and in paperback; it is a book of festering green skies, haiku, star boats and emotional androids.

Wendy is also the author of the scifi novel "Pale Zenith" (Eye Scry Publications) and its accompanying two-story volume, "Moltenrose." Her short story collection, "Beneath the Blue Dusk and the Sea" is also just out, as well as several male/male romances including a vampire-fairy novel, "Lace." She lives in the high desert of Yucca Valley, CA with her partner of 35 years, three dogs and three cats. She talks about writing and does mini-interviews with other authors at her blog, "From the Left Dimension"...
http://wendyrathbone.blogspot.com

LACE
Wendy Rathbone

Lace is a being from another dimension on Earth. He cannot die and humans call his kind "vampire" and declare war on them.

Firi is a human military soldier, a trained guard, who has met Lace twice in his young life and formed a bond with him.

In a world where humans and vampires are arch enemies, where vampires are eradicated in horrible ways, where being a vampire-lover means a death sentence, can Firi and Lace ever find each other again and explore the feelings they have for each other?

Will Lace be able escape his government prison, and the amnesia that keeps him from accessing his true powers?

Can Firi, the boy he met in the woods ten years ago, ever hope to help him?

A male/male romance about secrets that can get you killed, impossible rescues, and old lovers who cannot be trusted.

On Amazon
www.facebook.com/groups/Carlos.Castaneda.group/

From the Author
www.eyescrypublications.com

SCOUNDREL
Wendy Rathbone

Antares is a willing sex slave, trained in the harems of Anada since the age of 18, and owned by a wealthy master who spoils his slaves. But all that changes when Empire soldiers invade Antares' world and he is taken away from the only life he's ever known.

In a colonized galaxy where starships are as common as houseflies, and a dark Empire seeks to control thousands of civilized worlds, there are those who fall through the cracks and refuse to be conquered, including the pirate, Slate, and his crew.

Out in the darkness of the unknown, among Empire soldiers and scoundrels, will bad fates befall Antares and his fellow captive companions?

Will Slate finally find the love he's been looking for his whole life?

Can Slate and Antares ever see eye to eye?

On Amazon
http://www.amazon.com/Scoundrel-Wendy-Rathbone-ebook/dp/B014BU7V42/ref=asap_bc?ie=UTF8

From the Author
http://www.eyescrypublications.com

LETTERS TO AN ANDROID
Wendy Rathbone

Cobalt is a created human, vat grown and born adult, with no human rights and indentured to serve others for the duration of his life. Liyan is a young man with wanderlust in his eyes, embarking on a career that takes him to the furthest regions of space. The two become unlikely friends and create a memorable long-distance correspondence. Through Liyan, Cobalt gets to explore the universe, living vicariously through his friend's wave transmissions. A strong bond develops between them that not even the stars can put asunder.

———————————————

Now you know an android who writes poetry.

This is all your fault. Did you not read my last wave telling you extracurricular activities for my kind are discouraged? Of course this is harmless and strangely enjoyable and does not necessarily require me to leave the hotel. Pel would not care if I wrote lines of equations or nonsensical juxtaposed words. As long as the act does not bring my mental state into question.

However, in history, poetry is often written by the rebels.

So we can keep this to ourselves.

Let me know about your lieutenant's test.

And to give you peace of mind, I never believed you observed me as anything other than human.

Some people are and always will be hateful bigots. Most people are simply uncomfortable in speaking to "property." And anyway, friendship, like poetry, is also discouraged.

Your friend,
Cobalt

FROM THE AUTHOR:
www.eyescrypublications.com

ON AMAZON:
http://www.amazon.com/Letters-Android-Wendy-Rathbone/dp/0989693872/

PALE ZENITH

Wendy Rathbone
*A Science Fiction
Novel*

On a far-flung "Earth" in a parallel universe, two factions are fighting a decades-long psychic war. Young talented psychics are being temporarily kidnapped from present day Earth, seemingly at random, to serve as part of one side's psychic army. They are put under the control of spychiatrists, mysterious machines with many limbs that have a programmed ability to travel time and space and universes to kidnap and control carefully selected humans. The humans never know they are being used; when their missions are completed they are brought back to their universe through time and placed back in their beds, their memories wiped.

––––––––––––––––

The shadows wound the tall corridor in muted gold, varnished brown. It seemed as though they were in the bowels of a giant serpent coiled outside time, outside space.

When they left the palace, a familiar sun flourished in a clear, blue sky. But this wasn't their sun. Not Zack's sun. It was an alien star burning within a different galaxy in an all too distant universe. Zack looked up squinting, trying to see if he could peer beyond the sky, beyond the pale of midday and into his own timespace, but there was nothing. Only sunlight. Only the thin atmosphere of an Earth not his own.

His back knotted again. Leo's presence was a gelid space inside his chest, empty. Always before he'd felt a warmth there, a sort of pressure like someone's hand pressed gently to his heart. He'd taken Leo for granted knowing, the way a shadow falls when you block the sun, that he was there around him, inside him: blood, air, salt, brain, soul. They were genetic duplicates, twins, spiritual halves. Without him, Zack knew the first icy tugs of panic.

FROM THE AUTHOR
www.eyescrypublications.com

On Amazon
http://www.amazon.com/Pale-Zenith-Wendy-Rathbone-ebook/dp/B00DRHMB00/ref=asap_bc?ie=UTF8

The Foundling
Wendy Rathbone

Diego is a powerful man with a tragic past. Out on the expansive ocean in his private yacht, he discovers a beautiful and mysterious man adrift on a raft, near death. The bond that forms between them in the aftermath of Alec's rescue is one of fierce passion, though lacking in trust. Can they make it work, or will Alec's amnesia bring forth secrets so disturbing as to tear them apart? A passionately erotic love story of desire and darkness, exquisite and explicit.

———————

I can see his struggle between gratitude and uneasiness. He is buffeted by all things new and strange. He does not know where he is from, who he is or what happened to him. He does not know me. There has not been enough time to transition between strangers and friendship.

This isolation of his is something I can identify with, but it is also a feeling no one can help him with until or unless he gets his own life back. And his memory.

If that doesn't happen, then it will take time for him to build a new life. He is polite to me, even friendly, but even a night together during a storm with his arms wrapped tight around my waist doesn't calm the surge I see inside him, the emptiness, the loss, possibly even panic. That night may have reinforced some trust in me, but so far not enough for him to completely relax.

He seeks me out, though. That's something. He sits by me at dinner when he can have any seat of his choosing. I watch him closely when he does not realize it. At dinner the following night after we had only 'slept' together, and before we go to bed again in separate rooms, I notice everything about him, how he moves, the way the air warms when he is closer to me, the dry sheen of his lips as they part for more air when he is reacting to something, or speaking, or eating.

His hands still shake. Anyone else might not notice because he keeps them clasped into fists at his sides or, while sitting, pressed tight to his lap.

I spend another fretful night alone. I dream restlessly, wild, loud and colorful visions I cannot recall at all as soon as my eyes open. All I know is the dreams leave me unfulfilled, impatient.

From the Author
www.eyescrypublications.com

On Amazon
http://www.amazon.com/Foundling-Wendy-Rathbone-ebook/dp/B008E97SOA/ref=asap_bc?ie=UTF8

None Can Hold the Dark

Wendy Rathbone

Book 2 in "The Foundling" Trilogy

"Why do you keep doing this illegal business?" Now Alec's gaze turned toward him, open as the day and lit with a sad frenzy, a challenge. "You could go anywhere, do anything, be anyone."

Diego had asked himself that question on rare occasions. In truth, he got used to what he was, what he did. Even a dangerous known was perhaps preferable to the unknown. "People depend on me."

Alec shook his head, but smiled a little as he said, "That's so weak." He leaned forward, over the arm of the chair, and put his shaking hand on the back of Diego's head. The kiss was cool, lingering, moist with salt. When Alec pulled back, he said almost matter of factly, "It's like there's sharks and there's goldfish and one can't decide to become the other."

Diego was still stunned by the kiss. But the words hit him hard. In them was the unfair conjecture of a locked fate. He believed in making his own fate...or luck. Did Alec think only one kind of man lived inside him and that was all there was to it? To life? It hurt. Badly.

Diego sat back on his heels, catching himself with his hands on the smooth floor. "So, Alec, which am I?"

Alec frowned.

Diego said, "I made choices in my life. I made them No one made them for me. If I need to be strong I'm strong. If I need to be vicious I can be that too. So what? I'm stuck there? In a pattern, a role...with no free will?"

Alec watched him inquisitively now.

"Because," Diego went on, "I'm solely responsible for my actions. Me. Could you say the same of the shark?"

They both waited, the silence covering them in muggy discomfort.

"You think you understand me?" Diego finally asked.

The Lostling: Alec's Story

Book Three in The Foundling Trilogy
Wendy Rathbone

The Lostling takes place directly after *None Can Hold the Dark*, as Alec and Diego relocate to San Francisco. There, amid salty winter wind and fog, Alec's lost memories slowly return and he must relive some of his most painful and terrifying moments to regain his forgotten self. In agonizing dreams and flashes of memory, he finally remembers what happened to him... and why.

Excerpt: *Putting a hand on his arm or leg, I can always feel the tremor of Diego even through his clothes, an innate wildness, a life-power.*

I always believed, from the first day Diego found me unconscious and dying, floating in the middle of a sapphire Caribbean ocean, there was a core of me unhidden, unforgotten, that cried out silently to the air and everything around me communicating who I am, what I am.

I can't remember it myself. Not that core, not anything up to the day I awoke in Diego's bed, sick and panicked. In that moment, I remembered nothing more than my first name, and even that memory is suspect. But this core of me demands to take things into its own hands to be seen, to make sure it remains "I am."

I believe Diego saw it, the urgent desperation in me wanting to be witnessed, and he made a promise to that essence of me, to that heart of me, that he would see me through anything that came my way. Something in me reached up and latched onto him, a clasping energy, and Diego clasped back.

It caught and held him. He was moved. He was compelled. He was mesmerized.

From the Author
www.eyescrypublications.com

On Amazon
http://www.amazon.com/Lostling-Alecs-Story-Foundling-Book-ebook/dp/B00RO8GSUW/

UNEARTHLY
Wendy Rathbone

*A Collection of
Award-Winning
Poetry*

Intro by the Author:
This book contains
all my out of print
chapbooks (mini-
collections of an
author's work
usually published by
smaller presses.)

The chapbooks published within include:

Moon Canoes, published by Dark Regions Press, 1994

(Im)mortal, published by Shadowfire Press, 1996

Scrying The River Styx, published by Anamnesis Press, 1999

Autumn Phantoms, published by Flesh and Blood Press, 2000

Dreams of Decadence Presents: Wendy Rathbone, published by DNA Publications 2002

Dancing in the Haunted Woodlands, published by Yellow Bat Review, 2003

Vampyria, published by Eye Scry Publications, 2005

She Sleeps With Vampires

She sleeps with vampires
courting velvet breaths
poem-dreams
chill-stopped hearts

Wrapped in her arms
like teddy bear thoughts
purple lips trembling
at her quiet throat
they love her more than
somber rain
more than autumn
more than ash-soft hearths of night.

FROM THE AUTHOR
www.eyescrypublications.com

ON AMAZON
http://www.amazon.com/Unearthly-Wendy-
Rathbone-ebook/dp/B00B0MTIZK/

Other titles from Eye Scry Publications...

SONS OF NEVERLAND
an erotic vampyre
novel
Della Van Hise

*"The virtuosity shown
here is only the
beginning of a
pyrotechnic talent
unfolding into the
hidden dimensions of
the human and
nonhuman spirit."*
-Jacqueline
Lichtenberg

"What Sons of Neverland resembled to me was the
creative hagiographies of Nikos Kazantzakis, where a few
stylized characters deliver a message that goes way
beyond the parameter of the characters themselves. And
much like Kazantzakis, this book zones on the question
of immortality. However, this is not just the decadent
historical immortality of the long-lived vampire, it is
immortality as a change in one's perception. This is the
story behind the story, delivered by characters that are
hyper-real - each one loaded with symbolism. Sons of
Neverland will have you filled, even brimming over with
the sense of Mysterium Tremendum et Fascinans. Go
there for a full helping of the numinous."
(A Reviewer on Amazon!)

Set against a backdrop of contemporary culture, SONS OF NEVERLAND explores the universal questions of life & death, sex & love - the most crucial challenges every human being faces - through the eyes of the immortal vampire.

_____

The novella "Kiss of the Black Angel" is available for free on Smashwords – a preview to SONS OF NEVERLAND.

From the Author:
www.eyescrypublications.com

On Amazon

www.amazon.com/Sons-Neverland-Della-Van-Hise-ebook/dp/B00O4GUH2W/

Prince of Umberlight
Alexis Fegan Black

"If Prince of Umberlight doesn't rattle your cage, you're more dead than the undead!"
-Night Readers

Thorn may be an 800 year old vampire, but he does not possess the ability to create others of his kind, and so he is cursed to fall in love with mortals, only to watch them grow old and die. Torn by grief, Thorn denounces his immortality and enters into a comatose oblivion for decades. When he awakens, he is no longer in London, but finds himself in a world spun into being by his own desires - a world where Time and Death do not exist, a world where it is forever autumn, where the Parish of Shadows and the River of Stars become his home. It is in this world of Umberlight that he meets Atom - an interloper into his private sanctuary, but also an impudent imp who is destined to reveal to Thorn the three dangerous elements a vampire must possess in order to become a Creator.

The Art of Brutality.
Submission to Dark Desire.
Love.

FROM THE AUTHOR
www.eyescrypublications.com

ON AMAZON
http://www.amazon.com/Prince-Umberlight-Tales-Book-ebook/dp/B00TRD2EHS/ref=asap_bc?ie=UTF8

NO FORWARDING ADDRESS
Della Van Hise

*When Terrans came to sail
dark seas,
And see what stars might
be...
Heaven moved with no
forwarding address,
And left this void to me.*
(Children's song from
Lazali)

————————

A literary science fiction novel told in the voice of an empath, *No Forwarding Address* explores the lures and the dangers of love, the tragedies and triumphs stirring in the human heart.

When Crystal and Raine first meet, it is 50 years after The Great War on Earth. They are hesitant to trust, afraid to love. But even if they are able to overcome these seemingly insurmountable obstacles, is even love enough?

When a man has the stars in his eyes, legend says he must serve them above all others.

————————————

I knew then that it wasn't love and hate who were mirror twins. The final irony was that <u>grief</u> would always turn out to be the paradoxical antithesis and simultaneous manifestation of whatever it is that humans call love.

Crystal remained silent and walked a few steps away from Raine – further down the shoreline, until she stood under the wing of one fallen Phantom. She thought of the ship she had seen from the balcony of our home, and though it had long since disappeared over the dark and treacherous abyss of the ocean, its image lingered clearly in her thoughts. On that ship was a man, she thought. A terribly lonely man who made no great difference to the flow of time or the memory of the galaxy. A man who, like Raine, was compelled to keep moving and look only ahead and never behind. A man who could not afford the luxury of waving goodbye to friends on shore.

At last, she turned toward her beloved and watched him watching the darkness. He stood only a few feet away, yet the images in my mind said he might as well have been a million light years off in the void. He was lost to her in that instant out-of-time, just as lost and impossible to find as the light from that ship which had vanished over the horizon...

From the Author
www.eyescrypublications.com

On Amazon
www.amazon.com/Forwarding-Address-Della-Van-Hise-ebook/dp/B00PEOSKJ0/

COYOTE
Della Van Hise

When River Willows is accused of a murder she didn't commit, her life takes a turn toward the sanctuary of a world existing at right-angles to our own. Combining the mysticism of martial arts and the romantic conflict of a young woman torn between two powerful men, COYOTE takes the reader on an epic journey of dangerous secrets, military cover-ups, and the infinite heart of the peaceful warrior.

_____

"So who's Coyote?" I asked, trying to ignore the effect he was having on me. "You?"

Steale laughed easily, though it did little to hide the torment behind that mask of indifference he wore so well.

"Coyote's a scavenger, Jack of all trades. The Native Americans call him the trickster - the one who brought chaos down on the world." He shrugged as if altogether unconcerned. "Original sin."

"Is that what you are?" I asked, keeping it light despite the growing knot my stomach. "Original sin?"

He kept his profile to me, eyes straight ahead as he drove. "Sure you want to know?"

I couldn't help wondering if I had cornered the coyote, or if the clever trickster had cornered me.

_____

From the author:
www.eyescrypublications.com

On Amazon
http://www.amazon.com/Coyote-Della-Van-Hise/dp/0976689782/

TEACHINGS OF THE IMMORTALS
Mikal Nyght

So... You Want To Live Forever?

The teachings are presented as brief vignettes in no particular order of importance. This is not a book you read from start to finish in a single night. It is a grimoire of self-creation, intended to be contemplated slowly so as to be assimilated wholly. Pick it up and turn to a page at random. Where your eyes come to rest on the page is your lesson for the day. Go no further until you have assimilated the lesson totally.

The teachings are seduction as much as instruction. This is the way of The Dark Evolution.

The Ruby Slippers

The danger of the consensual continuum is that its natural gravity exists at the lowest common denominator of human experience, and because of this it will automatically make you forget those elusive truths you've fought to learn, and before you know it you're lost in petty dramas again, sinking into the mire of old familiar scripts.

The only way to overcome this is to be continually cavorting with worlds and events beyond human experience, journeying into the unknown so that it can become known, expanding knowledge and awareness to become more than you were, bringing back from the Dreaming those secrets which will teach you how to use the ruby slippers to transport yourself over the rainbow to the vampyre wizard's secret lair.

Perception

This is the nature of reality: to be precisely what perception dictates, as solid and whole as your interpretation of it, or as changeable and eternal as you permit it to be.

It wasn't knowledge god tried to keep from Man, you see. It was perception, for perception alone has the power to destroy god and obliterate comfortable consensual realities to create unending immortality.

Take the apple, my embryonic children. Nibble its red red flesh. Open your vampyre eyes so you may finally begin to *See*.

From the Author
www.immortalis-animus.com
www.eyescrypublications.com

On Amazon
www.amazon.com/Teachings-Immortals-Mikal-Nyght-ebook/dp/B00C2HY5WS/

Eye Scry Publications
A Visionary Publishing Company
www.eyescrypublications.com

www.ingramcontent.com/pod-product-compliance
Lightning Source LLC
Chambersburg PA
CBHW020549130626
46552CB00007B/2825

* 9 7 8 1 9 4 2 4 1 5 0 8 4 *